I0689523

AN ALIEN AFFAIR

AN ALIEN AFFAIR

DRAGON APPROVED™ BOOK NINE

RAMY VANCE

MICHAEL ANDERLE

THE AN ALIEN AFFAIR TEAM

Thanks to the JIT Readers

Dave Hicks
Diane L. Smith
Kathleen Fettig
Veronica Stephan-Miller
John Ashmore
Deb Mader
Kelly O'Donnell
Dorothy Lloyd

If we've missed anyone, please let us know!

Editor
The Skyhunter Editing Team

This Book is a work of fiction. All of the characters, organizations, and events portrayed in this novel are either products of the author's imagination or are used fictitiously. Sometimes both.

Copyright © 2020 by Ramy Vance & Michael Anderle
Cover Art by Jake @ J Caleb Design
http://jcalebdesign.com / jcalebdesign@gmail.com
Cover copyright © LMBPN Publishing
A Michael Anderle Production

LMBPN Publishing supports the right to free expression and the value of copyright. The purpose of copyright is to encourage writers and artists to produce the creative works that enrich our culture.

The distribution of this book without permission is a theft of the author's intellectual property. If you would like permission to use material from the book (other than for review purposes), please contact support@lmbpn.com. Thank you for your support of the author's rights.

LMBPN Publishing
PMB 196, 2540 South Maryland Pkwy
Las Vegas, NV 89109

First US Edition, April 2020
eBook ISBN: 978-1-64202-871-3
Print ISBN: 978-1-64202-872-0

DEDICATION

For Orla Julia Sim Habeeb – the little alien in my life.

—Ramy

*To Family, Friends and
Those Who Love
to Read.
May We All Enjoy Grace
to Live the Life We Are
Called.*

— Michael

The Wasps Nest was a marvel of modern technology and magic. The design had been Myrddin's-he was the wizard who had dedicated his life to the destruction of the Dark One—and the technology used was his attempt to bring together what he'd seen humanity excel at with what he knew magic could do.

The Nest was unrivaled in any of the nine realms. True, there were races who could boast of their magical creations and artifacts, but there was nothing like Myrddin's project, a constantly growing, changing, and learning machine imbued with a magic that only Myrddin seemed to understand.

It hadn't been built for housing alien species or with decontamination in mind, but luckily, due to its ingenious design, it was prepared for the extraterrestrial guest. All that had been needed was a quick word between Myrddin and Roy to give the team enough time to plan.

That was why Alex had never seen this particular hallway or section of the Nest before. It was an alabaster medical bay split into two sections with a thick glass wall.

The alien was on one side of the glass, staring down at its

hands, apparently still disoriented. The extraction from the crash site had been rushed and uncomfortable. Even Alex thought Myrddin could have been more accommodating.

They were all acting like the alien was something to be afraid of, as if it didn't come to their world specifically to offer them help against the Dark One. Everyone was acting like they'd watched too many alien movies. Alex had never seen one, but she had often listened in on her dad watching them.

Science fiction had been her father's favorite genre, and anything to do with the subject of aliens interested him. It got to the point where he'd once claimed he wished he would be abducted. Alex and her mom had teased him for years, telling him his dreams of being kidnapped by some extraterrestrial being were insane and it was never going to happen.

Dad would freak the hell out if he saw this, Alex thought as she stared at the alien through the glass. And he'd have an answer to his age-old question: yes, everyone in the universe *does* speak English.

She had to tell her dad about the most recent visitor. There was no way he would believe it. Luckily, Alex didn't have to rely on her word. She flipped up her HUD visor and started snapping pictures.

The alien looked up from his hands and stared at Alex. She suddenly realized how rude she was being and how frightening this experience must be. The alien was obviously annoyed that it was being treated like an invader.

Alex walked over to the glass and placed her hand on it, hoping it would understand.

Shouldn't be too hard, she thought. *He obviously understood my words.*

As if it could read Alex's mind, the alien stood and approached the glass, resting its hand against it as well. They looked into each other's eyes.

Alex had seen a lot of strange things since she got her eyesight, but there was something very odd about the alien's eyes. The irises seemed to be constantly expanding and contracting. It was impossible, but Alex couldn't deny what she was seeing. It was not that its eyes were sunken or that they implied some kind of wisdom; rather, it was as if they were a portal into another world, one that stretched away to infinity and was filled with welcoming darkness.

Alex had to look away. Staring into the alien's eyes gave her the distinct feeling of falling and not being able to catch herself. She'd felt something like that while looking at Gill or Jim at times, but there was no emotion behind the sensation she was getting from the alien, just the physical feeling.

As Alex pulled away, Roy and Myrddin walked into the decontamination area. They were both wearing hazmat suits that looked almost laughable on them. Neither of them seemed to be joking, though.

The two men walked up and Myrddin waved his hand, causing the barrier to slide open enough for both of them to step through. They approached the alien, and the three began speaking together. The alien seemed to respond, but Alex couldn't be sure since she couldn't hear through the glass.

After a couple of minutes, Roy stepped out and pulled off his mask. "You were the one who found it, right?" he asked, breathing in as much fresh air as he could.

Alex peeked over Roy's shoulders to see what Myrddin and the alien were doing. "Yeah, with help from the rest of Team Boundless."

"You spoke to it. And touched the ship."

Alex thought back, trying to remember if any of the rest of the team had spoken to the alien. She wasn't sure, but she was very certain that she had touched the ship. It had been warm, almost as if it were alive. "Yeah, I did. Why?"

Roy pointed to the door he and Myrddin had come

through. "You're quarantined. Come on, follow me." He walked past Alex, only turning for a moment to motion for her to follow him.

Alex didn't bother asking why she was being quarantined. She'd worked with Roy enough to know he would tell her when he thought she was ready to hear. Besides, he was her commanding officer, even if he was a mech rider, and it hadn't been a suggestion.

Roy led Alex down a long hall to a room not much different than the one the alien was in. The glass door slid open, and Roy gestured that Alex should step inside. She did, and the door closed behind her. "Sorry about all that. Myrddin's orders."

Alex went over and sat down on the bench in the room. She could hear Roy perfectly, so it must have been different from the room the alien was being held in. "Kinda figured. I don't usually get sent to my room without a reason."

Roy rubbed off the sweat beading on his forehead and then scratched his stubbly five-o'clock shadow. "The old man's freaking out a little bit. I'll be back. Myrddin and I need to chat with you after this thing gets finished telling us what it's doing here."

"It's not a *thing*," Alex corrected, indignant at Roy and her situation.

Roy flung his arms up as he turned to leave. "Far as we know, this thing could be talking mold or an irradiated fingernail shaving. It's a thing until it lets me know whatever the hell it is. I'll be back, kid."

Roy walked off, shutting the door behind him as Alex jumped to her feet, shouting, "Could you at least leave me a book or something?"

It was too late. Roy didn't hear her, but the Nest did. The glass wall next to Alex opened up, and a leather-bound book shot out at Alex and fell to the ground. It was titled *All You Need to Know About Space*.

Alex groaned as she picked up the book and started flipping through it. *At least the Nest is starting to get a sense of humor*, she thought.

For the next two hours, Alex read through the book. It was dry, lacked any wit, and seemed to have an ever-expanding, nonsensical idea about outer space. The more Alex read, the more she was convinced that the author should not write anything on any subject.

Once Alex's irritation peaked and solidified, she tossed the book across the room and gave a frustrated groan. Why the hell was she the one locked up? It wasn't like *she* came from space. Sometimes it felt like Myrddin and Roy were punishing her for doing her job.

The glass door slid open, and both Roy and Myrddin walked into the quarantine room. Both of them were still wearing their hazmat suits. As they walked toward Alex, a faint mist that smelled of lilacs sprayed throughout the room. "What's with the mist?"

Myrddin took a seat on the bench and pulled off his mask. "Just a precaution. We need to make sure we're going about this the right way. Alex, when did you first see the ship?"

Not even a hello. *Wow*, she thought before answering Myrddin. "Around early evening. I don't know, maybe five-thirty?"

Roy narrowed his eyes at Alex. "What were you doing in that area?"

"Why am I the one on trial right now? Isn't it a good thing I reported a strange thing in the sky? And I'll have you know, it was my day off, so I went on a date."

Roy patted Alex on the back as he chuckled. "Glad to hear you were making the most of your leave time. Not everyone knows how to spend it. Some of those nerds read on their days off. Who was the lucky—"

Roy trailed off as he turned to see Myrddin staring daggers in his back. "Uh, I meant, good thing you didn't forget your duty to report things."

Myrddin folded his hands together as the lines in his forehead became more pronounced. "You are not in trouble, Alex. We're only asking because this is unexpected."

Alex hadn't ever heard Myrddin admit to being caught off-guard before. She let go of her anger and let her curiosity take over. "What do you mean unexpected? Is that thing a for-real alien? Like, from another planet?"

Myrddin shook his head as he kneaded his forehead wrinkles. "When there are nine realms, each with their own universe, the term 'alien' stops having any real meaning. Humans are alien to elves, and so on and so forth. But this creature is something else entirely. It's not from our dimension."

"Wait, you mean like the meteor? That thing that had the Dark One's persona or essence in it?"

Myrddin reached out to the wall, which opened, letting a tray with a cup of iced water pass through. "Similar to it. It's from the same dimension, but it came here in a conventional fashion. That's why you and it are quarantined for the moment. We can't risk there being an interdimensional virus or something that our bodies aren't used to. It should be fine, but we need to be safe."

Alex didn't want to think about the meteor. But if this thing was from the same dimension as the Dark One, there was a good chance it had witnessed what he was capable of firsthand. "So, why's it here?"

"We were only able to get a little information. The creature referred to the Dark One as the Devourer of Worlds, and it meant that quite literally. I don't quite know what to make of that, but the creature fell asleep shortly after. We plan on speaking with it more tomorrow. We will be examining the ship as well."

"Great. Thanks for the check-in. Anything else I should know?"

Myrddin and Roy exchanged glances. "Guess I'll tell her," Roy said, sighing. "You're going to have to spend the night here. And most of tomorrow. Just to be safe."

Alex groaned and sat back down on the bench. "Are you kidding me? All night?"

Myrddin and Roy were heading to the door. The old man looked over his shoulder. "If you need anything, the wall will help. But be very specific. I'm still working the kinks out. Thank you again, Alex."

They left Alex alone with her thoughts. Even though she tried to fight it, her mind inevitably turned to the meteor and what she had seen within it. *Nope,* Alex thought. *No nightmares tonight.*

Alex focused on what she wanted: company. She closed her eyes and imagined Jollies' smiling face. When she opened them, the wall next to her had built a holoprojector and Jollies' comm frequency was ready to be dialed. After a quick ring, Jollies picked up. "Hello?"

Alex sighed in relief. "Thank God. It's me, Alex."

"What are you calling me from? What happened to your comm?"

"It's a long story, but I'm in quarantine."

Jollies popped up on the holoscreen. She was brushing her teeth. "Long story? Good. I'm all ears," she giggled.

They talked for a long time, then Alex went to sleep.

CHAPTER TWO

Alex awoke in the middle of the night. She felt like she couldn't breathe, and her heart was pounding fast enough to crack her rib cage. Sweat poured from her brow. Worst of all, she wasn't sure if she was herself.

Her fear had been growing since the night after she destroyed the meteor that had come rocketing through the sky a few weeks ago. The first night after the mission, Alex'd had a nightmare, a rarity for her. Even as a child, she'd rarely had nightmares. That had changed recently.

The nightmares were never understandable. They were not like dreams. She didn't find herself repeating her experience of the meteor, nor did her mind take past experiences and layer them on top of that one horrifying episode.

Instead, Alex dreamed of a color that permeated her mind like some kind of gas, staining the inside of her skull, leaking out of her skin, and submerging her eyes until they were a deep, awful green. Alex felt the color crawling up her body like living slime, covering her from head to toe, and then stretching out toward her friends, toward the end of the universe.

It was this dream, recurring nearly every night, that Alex awoke from. She rubbed her eyes, trying to remind herself that she had a body. That she was not some abstract interplay of light and darkness. That she had weight to her. By the time she was comfortable again, she felt stupid. It was obvious she wasn't a color.

As she pulled back the blankets supplied by the magical hole in the wall, she wondered why she had started having these dreams. Obviously, she'd been shaken up by what had happened on the meteor. Anyone would have been. The whole thing had seemed like a bad acid trip, or at least what she'd heard that was like.

Yet Alex felt it was something more than the disturbing nature of her experience. She felt that if she were just dreaming about that, then it would have been more focused, not this vague feeling of dread about becoming green.

The Nest needs to hire a therapist. You rarely heard about that or saw it in war or science fiction movies, except for Troi on the Enterprise, Alex mused as she leaned back on the pillow mattress she'd built atop the glass bench.

As she tried to shake the last bit of sleep from her head, she imagined herself in a coffee shop, reading a book that would take some of the edge off her nightmare. She turned to the magical hole in the wall and took the steaming coffee that appeared alongside a copy of *The Interpretation of Dreams* by Carl Jung.

Alex had heard the name before, although psychology had never been an interest of hers. But if it was going to help her better understand her dreams, it was worth a try.

The next few hours dragged by as Alex powered through the first chapters of the book, sipping coffee. She had no idea what time it was but also didn't want to check. Obsessing about how much longer quarantine was going to last sounded like about as fun as finishing Jung's book.

She could see why she didn't like to read psychology. It was filled with terms and concepts she'd never encountered. The book read like a foreign language. Further, it made her tired, and sleeping was the last thing Alex wanted to do.

That didn't matter, though, because she drifted off to sleep in her third hour of reading. She woke up screaming from the same recurring dream. Waking up this time was much more violent since Alex had thrown herself off the bench and was tangled up in her blankets.

By the time she got untangled, she was panting and trying to catch her breath. She tossed the blankets back onto the bench and turned to find Jim staring at her through the glass. She smiled sheepishly, attempting to play it off as if she were doing something perfectly normal.

Jim had a picnic basket, a bottle of pop, and his adorable smile. He was also dressed very nicely in a collared shirt and paisley tie with tan chinos. He knocked politely. "Mind if I come in? We still have a date to finish."

Alex walked up to the glass and tapped on it. "I'm quarantined if you hadn't noticed. I don't think you're even allowed to be in the same building as me."

Jim held a piece of paper up to the glass that read Free of Alien Disease. "I got quarantined too and got my all-clear," Jim said. "Myrddin figures that if I'm clean, you probably are too. But just in case, we're to stay on this level. I asked if I could tell you the good news and…well, um… So, you wanna finish our date?" He held out the blanket.

Alex spread her arms wide, motioning that there was more than enough space for Jim. The glass door slid open, and he stepped inside her prison. He looked around, nodding as he appraised the room. "I like what you've done with the place. It's got a European flair to it."

Alex playfully shoved the mech rider as she walked past

him to sit on the bench. "Shut up. What did you bring, anyway?"

"Some snacks. Figured it had been a while since you'd eaten anything. They kinda forgot to feed me while I was locked up. You would have thought I got sent to prison or something."

"You didn't use the magic wall?"

Jim raised an incredulous eyebrow at Alex before she leaned over to the magical hole in the wall and took out a pulled pork sandwich. "No," Jim exclaimed, his eyes wide. "I would have definitely used that if I'd known about it."

Alex offered the sandwich to him.

"Yeah, it's this new thing Myrddin was working on, I guess. It's kinda freaky, but I don't know, pretty convenient. But anyway, let's take care of this food."

The two dug into the assortment of snacks Jim brought, demolishing them quickly before turning to the magical hole in the wall. They thought of whatever they could to satisfy the hunger that had been awakened in both of them from grapes and apple slices.

As the two ate from the treasure trove of junk food they'd supplied themselves with, Jim noticed the Jung book on the floor. "I don't know you were into Jungian psychology," he mused.

Alex grabbed the book and threw it onto the pile of blankets behind her. She didn't want to talk about her dreams. She'd just started to feel normal again. "Oh, that was the wall screwing up what I was looking for."

"Oh? What were you looking for?"

Alex couldn't think fast enough, caught in her badly thought-out lie. "Uh, I don't know anything about Jung or psychology, but I was trying to find something about dreams. You know, like how to interpret them."

"Gotcha. I only asked because my mom has tons of that

stuff lying around. She's a Jungian therapist. I've read a couple of his books just 'cause they're everywhere in the house, but I don't understand most of it. The dream one is a little easier, though. It made some sense."

"Do you ever have nightmares?"

Jim looked taken aback by the question. His brow furrowed. "Why do you want to know?"

Alex thought Jim's response was odd. Usually he was fairly candid, but Alex noticed that he had thrown up a wall in a matter of seconds. "Is that a weird question?"

"A little bit. Most people ask what you dream about, not what you have nightmares about."

"I didn't ask what you had nightmares about. I wanted to know if you ever had any."

Jim still looked uncomfortable, but he finally answered. "I didn't use to have nightmares, even when I was a kid. But recently, yeah, I've been having them. Really bad ones, too. The weird thing is that when I wake up, I don't think what I'm dreaming about is even remotely scary. It's...I don't know...like a..."

"Color. Is it a nightmare about a color?"

Jim glanced up from his food, his bottom lip trembling. He looked as if someone had told him how he was going to die; his face was pale. "How did you know?"

Alex tapped the side of her head. "Because I've been having the same dream almost every night. Just this green color."

"Like from the meteor?"

"Exactly."

Alex and Jim exchanged glances. How was this even possible? Jim was the first one to try to offer an explanation. "It must be from what we saw, you know," he stammered. "That green stuff with the meteor was pretty weird."

"It was more than weird, Jim."

"People don't have the same dreams."

Alex didn't know why she wasn't convinced by what Jim was saying. Minutes ago, she'd been telling herself that her color dreams weren't strange. Hearing Jim act like everything was okay was casting light on the situation's unnaturalness.

Jim was still trying to explain away what they had both just realized. "We went through a traumatic experience together. Of course, we're going to have similar dreams. People who fight in the same battles or war or whatever probably dream the same crap—the color red and everything."

"I don't think this is the same thing, Jim."

Jim looked as if he were ready to run out of the room. His fear was palpable. He had the gaze of a small animal, something that realizes it is prey and its life is not its own. Whatever was going on deeply disturbed him. Alex could see it in his haunted eyes.

The silence stretching between them was broken by the crackling of the intercom and Alex's dragon anchor roaring to life. "Alex, we need you in Bay Seven."

"Bay Seven? We have a Bay Seven?"

There was an audible sigh. "Does no one go over the site maps anymore? It's Level Seven, directly below where you are. Bring Jim as well."

Alex sighed, irritated that she wasn't going to get a moment to finish the conversation. "Well, you heard the man," Alex muttered as she walked past Jim, who was still rooted to the spot, his eyes distant as if he were dreaming while standing. "Hey! Jim!" she shouted.

Jim snapped back to reality. "Sorry. Let's go."

Part of the docking bay had been converted to a quarantine area, and that was where the alien's ship was. Myrddin and Roy were next to the ship with the technicians who were looking it over.

Roy waved Alex and Jim over when he saw them enter. "Glad to see you two didn't catch any alien cooties," he joked.

"Was there anything to catch?"

Roy mimed spiders running over his forearms as he nodded. "Oh, yeah, definitely. We picked up a handful of microbes that don't exist in this reality. Luckily for us, they don't seem to interact with our molecular structure. It would be like if you sneezed on an ant. Doesn't do shit, you know?"

If there was something Alex knew nothing about, it was interdimensional physiology. "So, you brought us down here to check out the ship?" Alex asked, trying to bring the conversation back to something rooted in her world.

Myrddin, who was hunched over, asked, "Would you please come closer?"

Alex and Jim came over. "How different from the meteor you saw is this ship?"

It always came back to the foul thing that had rocketed through the sky and nearly destroyed the planet. Something like the Dark One had been inside. It had crept into Alex's mind, and she knew now that it was responsible for her dreams. Even though they'd managed to destroy the meteor and the bit of the Dark One or whatever the hell it was inside it, something still lingered.

Or at least Alex thought something was lingering. She didn't know what it could have been. The meteor had been destroyed. She'd blown it up herself.

Yet the color, the green shade—where did that come from, the color in her nightmares?

"Alex!"

Myrddin's voice pulled Alex away from her thoughts.

"They're nothing alike," she finally said. "This is a ship. The meteor was more like a living hive, and the whole thing felt like a hallucination. You remember my briefing about the child being in the mind of the hive. It was nothing like this."

Myrddin stood up as he continued to study the ship. "That was what I thought. You didn't mention any odd experiences when coming into contact with this ship," he mused.

"What does that mean for us? And our alien friend?"

"For us? It means this didn't come from the Dark One's planet. His dimension but not his planet. For our friend? It means there are a lot more questions to be answered. You two are dismissed. Alex, I'd like you to stay one more night in quarantine, just to be safe. I'm not sure if Jollies' molecular structure can handle this dimension's radiation."

Alex was more than happy to have another night of solitude. The conversation she'd had with Jim about their dreams had unsettled her. "Sure, no problem. Oh, I almost forgot!"

Alex hit her dragon anchor and pulled out the black rod that had separated her and Chine's connection. "I got hit with one of these by a giant and it killed my connection with Chine. Thought you might want to take a look at this tech."

Myrddin gave the rod a quick glance. "I'll set you up with a communication device in your room. Contact Abby from Earth's HQ and have her run tests on the rod. If this is tech the Dark One has, we need to neutralize it as soon as possible."

"Sounds good to me."

Alex saluted Roy and Myrddin before turning to leave. She caught a glimpse of Jim out of the corner of her eye. He was deep in thought, staring at the alien's ship. As Alex turned around, she could have sworn she saw a flash of green light, but she couldn't be certain.

CHAPTER THREE

Back in quarantine, Alex pulled up the holoprojector installed in the wall while trying to remember what Abby looked like. They had only met once briefly. Team Boundless had been recruited at the last minute to help with a rescue mission Abby and the rest of the DGA, Dark Gate Angels, were working on.

When the mission was over, Abby and Alex had had a bit of time to talk, and once Alex realized Abby was a human teenager like her, they decided to stay in touch.

Now that Alex was calling Abby, she wished that they would be talking about something other than work, but a conversation was a conversation.

The holoprojector on the wall blinked as the call was being placed, then Abby's face popped up on the screen. She was wearing a white coat and thick glasses, her short dreads sticking out at odd angles. Behind the glasses, there were large dark circles under her eyes, the sort you only get from long periods of time without sleep. "Hello?" she muttered

Alex waved at her and smiled brightly. "Hey, Abby, it's me, Alex. From the dragonriders, remember?"

Abby pushed up her glasses and yawned widely before returning the smile. "Of course! How are you doing? I was thinking about calling you today, actually."

"I'm not too bad. I'm sort of in quarantine right now for coming across an alien ship. I seemed to be clear of any interdimensional microbes, but Myrddin doesn't want me mixing with the general population just in case."

Abby didn't seem fazed by the news that aliens existed. "Yeah, I know what you mean. Never a dull moment, saving Middang3ard."

"It was my day off, too. I've been cooped up for two days."

"Sounds terrible. I would have lost my mind by now. How are you keeping sane?"

Alex picked up her Jung book off of the floor. "A lot of reading. I've been getting visitors too. The quarantine isn't too bad. At least I don't have to worry about being sent on a mission while I'm here."

"True, true."

Alex held up the black rod she'd gotten from the giant. "Sorry, but I had to call on business. There's something I need analyzed if you have time."

Abby lowered her glasses and stared at the rod through the holoprojector. "No problem. Figured you were as busy as I am. Lemme see what I can do. Can you send it over?"

Alex wondered if she could. Myrddin didn't seem to have thought it was a problem when he'd told Alex to share her discovery with Abby. "Maybe, " Alex murmured as she tried to think of the right thing to concentrate on. She didn't know how bases traded information or objects like this, so Alex focused on Abby getting the rod.

When Alex opened her eyes, the wall in front of her had contorted so that there was a glowing pad before her. Seemed simple enough. Alex placed the black rod on the pad, which turned light pink before transporting the rod. Then the pad sucked itself back in.

Abby turned around onscreen, looking over her shoulder. "Okay, looks like I got it. Anything you can tell me about it?"

Alex wrapped her feet in the blankets lying on the floor. "Not really. All I know is that a giant aimed it at me and it shut down all my gear. I couldn't even hold onto my dragon."

Abby held the black rod up to the screen. "I can see why that would have you worried. I'll take a look at it and call you if I figure anything out. It was nice seeing you again."

"Thanks for taking a look for me. And it was good to see you again."

Abby waved quickly, and the video cut out. Back to her little room of isolation. She decided to read a bit more and see if there was something in the Jung book to help her. It was easier to understand, but most of the information was way above Alex's head. There was nothing more boring than trying to educate yourself when you were trapped.

Alex decided to take a break. She leaned close to the wall, imagining a large iced soda and a cheeseburger with extra onions and pickles. The hole coughed the food up, and Alex sat down on the floor to eat while she wrote a letter to her parents.

Since arriving back from the last mission within the meteor, Alex hadn't spoken with her folks much, not after reassuring them that she was alive and well. Finding time to write a letter with her class load and training was hard enough. That, coupled with not wanting to give her parents any cause to worry, was enough to put Alex off writing a letter. There was no way she was going to tell them she'd lost an arm.

That brought up the question of what they needed to know. Alex did not like thinking about communicating with her parents in that way. It felt dishonest, like a double life, but what other choice did she have? Her mom and dad weren't military like Jim's parents. They had been reluctant to let her come to Middang3ard to begin with. If they found out how much danger she was in, they'd probably demand that she come back home.

Could Alex even go home? The criteria for her service had never been explicitly stated. From what she could tell, everyone who had been helping Myrddin had been doing it for a long time, but it didn't seem like he was keeping anyone here contractually.

Alex figured it was because people believed what they were doing mattered. The Dark One's mind, or at least part of it, had been laid open to Alex. There was no way she could go back to living a regular life with that thing out there.

Once Alex started writing, the information her parents needed to know flowed out.

Dear Mom and Dad,

Sorry it's taken me so long to write to you. I've been really busy. Like, you have no idea how busy. Anyway, I don't want to bore you with all the military stuff, but here are some of the highlights.

So, you should know because I'm going to keep talking about it. Jim and I went on a date. Now, I don't want to make a big deal out of it, but before you ask, Mom, it was soooooo magical. And before you ask, Dad, he was a perfect gentleman.

There were fairies and a picnic and everything. It was nice to hang out with another human. Not that I don't like hanging out with everyone, but it gets a little lonely, not being able to talk about TV or junk like that sometimes. Look at me, right, talking to people about TV. Now that I can see, I watch TV. Who would have thought? Between you and me, I wasn't missing much.

Other than that, things have been pretty exciting. I'm doing well in my studies, and the missions I've been on have all been successful. I have my own team and everything. Also, my roommate is amazing. She's a pixie and a little spitfire. I think you both would love her. But anyway, let me know how you guys are doing? I know we can have visitors here if you ever want to see what my new home is like. Let me give you a heads up: it is very weird. Send me a chunky letter to read! Seriously.

I love you both so much,

Alex

She considered telling her dad about the alien but decided against it. Not now, not until they knew more about who or what the creature was.

Once Alex was done with the letter, she emailed it to her parents.

Alex checked the time. It was still pretty early in the evening, but the cheeseburger had put her in a food coma. Sleep was coming for her, regardless. She didn't complain, though. The last few days had been exhausting, and she still didn't feel like she'd gotten a decent night's sleep.

And it was nice, not hearing Jollies' snoring. Alex still didn't understand how such a small pixie was able to produce so much noise.

Alex grabbed the pillows and blankets off the floor and tossed her leftovers into the wall's hole. Then she cuddled up on the bench, snuggling her face into the pillow until she could hardly breathe and her face was hot.

That was how she drifted to sleep.

The earth was soft. Something was chirping, she didn't know what. The inside of her mouth was as soft as velvet, learning itself, the back of her teeth soft and malleable.

Alex's hands reached up out of the earth. She'd been

buried but did not know by whom or where. It could have been anywhere, but it was a smell that woke her up, which sent her fingers searching above the fertile womb earth that now birthed her, confused and bowlegged.

Forward she went into the darkness, which was lacquered thick and heavy with the scent of flowers unseen and unknown. They were not from Earth. Alex could have identified them if they were from Earth.

Nor were they from Middang3ard. No, this was something else. It was not familiar.

Alex continued her search, her feet moving forward as if something was pulling her forward. She was a slow-moving arrow. There was a destination, and she moved toward it inevitably.

There was a crow cawing, a call that sent shivers down Alex's spine. She knew what was coming now. This was how it always happened.

She wasn't far from her birth canal. She could go back. It would be possible to find her way back.

Alex felt as if she always ran, no matter the reason or circumstance.

The crow stopped cawing. The air was now hot and humid, clinging like a second skin waiting to be peeled back.

The blackness sizzled and foamed above as if it were a plastic plate melting in a fire. It reeled back, and beneath was a streak of green light, filtering down like smoke, filling the sky. Every color was present, with a bright jade flame that threatened to engulf all.

Alex stood, watching the green insinuate itself into her universe. It did not care for the stars that fell like fruit once they were touched or crows whose eyes bulged like bugs when the green washed over them. The color brought silence, indifference. It made Alex's legs buckle under the weight of her fear.

She ran in no particular direction. The green was coming down around her. It didn't matter where she went.

And then the green began to pull back. It was running, hiding from something bright and loud down on the ground, not too far from Alex. She knew that was where she had to go. As she ran toward the sound and the light, the green pulled away.

The alien from the ship was basking in the light, its legs crossed, staring up at the green, singing loudly. It was driving the green away.

Alex stood there, watching the creature. She was very aware that she was not dreaming about the alien; it was *in* her dreams. "What are you doing here?"

The alien did not stop singing. It merely looked at the sky. Its eyes fastened on Alex and her brain slid out of this dream and into many others, all playing at the same time. There were many voices screaming in pain and agony, folk who looked like the alien, their bodies piled high in ditches as blood poured from the heavens in a great sheet.

Alex fell to her knees, covering her ears, trying to block the sound of so much pain. There were few words, but the ones Alex could make out were "the Dark One," over and over.

The crow began cawing again.

Alex snapped awake, gasping for breath. She was still in the quarantine room. It was a little after eight in the morning. Her dragon anchor was peeping, a message from Myrddin. "Quarantine is officially over. You may now mix with the general population. Come to the alien's room ASAP. He says he needs to speak with you."

CHAPTER FOUR

Alex was met by some scientists who supplied her with a change of armor. She followed them down the halls to the room that held the alien. Myrddin and Roy were standing on the other side of the glass, waiting for her.

The alien looked at Alex when she walked in. The same deep darkness was in its eyes, but Alex didn't feel the overwhelming sense of dread like before. Instead, she felt almost as if the eyes were inviting her to step closer, to engage in conversation. To listen and learn.

Myrddin motioned for Alex to come to his side. "He requested to speak to you by name," Myrddin informed Alex. "He identifies as male, by the way. We can stop saying 'it.'"

Alex wasn't surprised he wanted to talk to her. She had just been dreaming with him, she was certain now—not dreaming of, dreaming with. "Did he happen to give you a name?"

Myrddin shook his head. "He's refused to talk to anyone other than you. I guess he must have a different idea of 'take me to your leader' than we've seen in the movies. We'll be out here in case you need anything."

The glass slid open, and Alex stepped into the room. The alien stared at her but made no motion. The dragonrider took the initiative, walking over to the bench and sitting down next to him. "My name's Alex," she said as she extended her hand.

The alien took her hand and shook it with the familiarity of a human. "My name is Vardis. It is good to meet you properly."

"You were in my head last night, weren't you?"

"Yes, we found ourselves sharing the same dream. It was unexpected. Usually, my kind cannot dream with others of different realms, but with you, it was almost like your dream called out to me. I was within it before I realized."

Alex thought the order of what Vardis had said was backward. Her recollection of her dream was a little fuzzy, but she knew Vardis had pulled *her* into *his* dream. Maybe that was what people felt like when they shared dreams. She didn't have a context. "Why would I have done that?"

"It might have been reflexive. Perhaps being around someone you could dream with caused you to do it instinctively. But *how* is a more interesting question. You must have had contact with someone like me in the past, and you must have dreamed with them."

Alex knew exactly what Vardis was talking about. She had shared a dream with the Dark One within the meteor, and gotten lost in that brain essence of hatred. She could have carried something out with her. Lucky if it was the ability to dream with someone. "Myrddin said you weren't from the same planet as the Dark One."

Vardis nodded. His eyes looked murky as if they were losing themselves to thoughts that could not be held. "Not the same planet, but the same realm. But I can see that you know that already. Where I come from, nearly all sentient beings can share each other's dreams."

"Where are you from?"

Vardis looked somberly at Alex. "If I were to tell you, it would mean nothing. It is only able to be said in the common language of my people, and I am afraid that your consciousness would not understand. We speak in something like image forms when conversing about our heavenly bodies. It is the only way to properly describe them."

"That sounds really cool. I've never heard of anything like that before. But is that what you called me here to talk about? Myrddin said you called for me by name."

"That is true. I wished to know how you acquired the ability to dream. Based on what I've seen, my assumption was that the wizard was in charge here." Vardis paused, looking Alex over. "Yet it was you, a child with whom I can dream. I find that interesting. How did it happen?"

Alex looked over at Myrddin. She knew he was listening and she wasn't sure how much she should tell Vardis. No one knew what Vardis was doing here other than his vague promise to give them something that would stop the Dark One forever. He hadn't said anything else about the subject. For all they knew, this could be an elaborate trap.

But how could telling Vardis about her meeting with the Dark One's essence backfire? She hadn't learned anything important, hadn't walked away with pertinent information. All she had received from the Dark One were terrible nightmares.

Myrddin's voice popped into Alex's head. *Tell him whatever you think he should know.* It was so surprising that Alex nearly jerked off the bench. *Don't react too much,* Myrddin said telepathically. *But as of this moment, I don't see the need to be secretive about your fight with the Dark One.*

Alex thought back, *When did you start being telepathic?*

When it started being useful for you to know.

Alex turned her attention back to Vardis. "Uh, a while

back, a meteor fell here. We thought your ship was the same kind of thing. The meteor wasn't a rock, though, more like a giant hive filled with these weird monsters. And the Dark One. There was an essence of the Dark One, and I interacted with it. I went inside whatever that thing's mind was. That's how I acquired the ability to enter your dream."

"That would explain it. A truly unique skill amongst your kind. I believe even among wizards, it is rare."

Vardis leaned forward and stared at Myrddin. Alex wasn't sure if this was a challenge or something but it made her feel extremely uncomfortable. There was a weird vibe going on between Myrddin and Vardis. Alex didn't know how to answer Vardis. She had no idea what wizards were capable of.

"So, what are you doing here?" Alex asked.

"As I said," Vardis began, "I am here to—"

There was a loud boom in the distance, and the room quaked. Cracks shot through the barrier like bolts of lightning. Alex and Vardis were thrown to the floor. On the other side of the room, Myrddin waved his hand, and the glass separating him and Roy from Alex and the alien disappeared.

A screeching alarm blared through the quarantine area as Myrddin and Roy helped Alex and Vardis to their feet. "What the hell was that?" Alex asked as another boom set the room shaking again.

Myrddin conjured a HUD into existence and pulled it up over his eyes. "An explosion," he replied. "We're under attack on the east side of the campus."

Alex's heart jumped up in her chest. During the last invasion of the Nest, they had lost so many cadets. The image of their bodies stacked in the main hall while orcs massacred the unarmed teenagers was burned vividly into Alex's mind. It didn't seem as if it were ever going away.

This can't be happening again, Alex kept repeating to

herself as her feet went cold. The chill ran up her legs and nestled in her stomach, where it grew and grew, pinpricks of ice all up and down her skin.

The last few months of victorious missions faded away as if they'd never happened. There was only the invasion. The constant invasion. It had never stopped. Alex knew that now.

The tightness in Alex's chest was slight at first. There was no indication that it was growing until she found herself on her knees, gasping for breath. She couldn't hear anything other than the explosions and the screams of children, the trampling of feet running for life.

She felt something on her back. It was an orc, had to be. She whirled around, striking it with her robotic arm as hard as she could.

Myrddin stood over her, a magical barrier floating in front of him. The barrier was more badly cracked than the glass in the room. "Alex, what's happening?"

Alex opened her mouth to speak but only screams came out before she doubled over again, grabbing her head, trying to keep from slipping into the darkness that clawed at her from the inside.

Jollies was dead in her hands while orcs dragged Gill away. Brath was screaming and kicking as two orcs took hold of his arms and legs, ripping him apart. Jim was lying face-down in a pool of his own blood. They were all dead. All of them.

Alex leaped up and backed against the wall as tears rolled down her cheeks, and she kept shaking her head.

Myrddin stepped over to the rider. As he waved his hand over her head, mist came from his fingers, covering her.

The panic broke, and Alex hiccupped. She still didn't feel as if she were in her body, but at least there was some relief from the fear that had raced through her like poison and shut down her ability to think. "Are you okay?" Myrddin asked.

Alex shook her head as the panic began to rev itself back up. "No, no! I can't do this, I can't do this again."

Myrddin grabbed Roy and said, "Take Alex. I have to figure out what's going on."

Roy nodded gruffly as Myrddin vanished. He grabbed Alex gently by the arm and led her out of the room as quarantine scientists rushed in. The glass wall went back up, and Roy told the scientists to keep a watch on Vardis.

Alex wasn't as panicked as she had been minutes ago, but she still wasn't certain where she was. She knew Roy was taking her someplace, but she felt as if she were floating along in a dream. Hadn't Vardis been talking to her about dreaming? Maybe that was all this was—a dream.

But dreams weren't like this. Dreams didn't make sense, and they weren't nearly this horrifying. This was a nightmare. It had to be. There was no way this could be happening again.

The world froze. Alex could have counted the hairs on Roy's neck, and reality became more focused and clearer.

At the end of the hall was a young boy. He was as white as fresh snow and wore the mask of a buck deer with spreading antlers. He turned to face Alex but said nothing.

Then the world reeled back into motion, and the boy was gone.

Roy led Alex into a room no larger than a broom closet and flipped on the lights. He sat Alex down and took a seat beside her. "Are you holding up okay?"

Alex shook her head as her body trembled. "I don't know what's happening. I-I can't stop shaking. I can't—"

Roy took Alex's hand and held it tightly. "Breathe. You need to breathe," he said. "Concentrate on your breathing. Nothing else matters. Just focus on breathing."

Alex tried to follow his advice as best as she could. She

thought of inhaling and then exhaling, over and over. Slowly, her heart slowed its incessant hammering.

Roy let go of Alex's hand and leaned forward, his face covered by shadows as he spoke. "It gets easier. Doesn't feel like it, but it does—the stress."

"I can't do this. There's no way—"

Roy cut Alex off. "You *can* do this because you have to. If you don't, no one else will. It's that simple."

Roy stood up and offered his hand to Alex. "We all have to. Together. Are you with us?"

Alex pushed down the vomit threatening to creep up her throat. Roy was right. This was why she was here. Someone had to defend the realms from the Dark One. She'd done it before. She could do it again.

Alex took Roy's hand and stood. "Yeah. I'm a dragonrider. I'm with you."

CHAPTER FIVE

The main hall of the Nest was filled with cadets and recruits. There were more than Alex remembered; Myrddin must have stepped up his recruitment game. There was nearly three times the number of certified dragonriders than there had been during the last invasion. The mech rider corps had grown as well.

Alex wasn't staying in the main hall, though. She was only passing through with Roy. The two were heading to the war room for an officer briefing since she was no longer a cadet or a recruit. She led Team Boundless and would be needed for the planning stages of the assault.

As Alex walked past the recruits, she could see how young most of them were—only a little older than she was. There were still no other humans besides the mech riders, who were housed in a different facility. Alex wondered how they had arrived at the Nest so fast. Maybe Myrddin had known the attack was coming.

The two made their way to the war room, where Myrddin and the rest of the faculty were gathered. A round holoprojector in the middle of the room displayed a large scale map of the Nest and the surrounding area.

Toppinir was talking with Myrddin and politely nodded at Alex when she walked in. "Good to see you are out of quarantine. I was worried Myrddin was going to keep you there indefinitely."

Alex chuckled nervously. She was still uncomfortable with the attitude change that happened with teachers when she was in a combat situation and not in class. It was as if they forgot she was a student or preferred to remember that when it came to a fight, she was their equal in many ways.

There were faces in the room Alex was unfamiliar with. Many of them were older students, cadets who had recently become certified dragonriders. The age gap was noticeable since the other captains looked like they were in their early twenties. She hadn't seen any of them in classes before and wondered just how large the Nest was if it could house people she'd never seen.

Alex already knew that Boundless was the youngest certified team of dragonriders. She hadn't realized how young she was compared to the rest. Most of the older cadets were only a year or two older than her. It was hard to tell with elves, though. She still didn't have a good handle on what constituted adolescence for an elf.

The older captains were standing in a line near the projector. Alex looked around the room, hoping someone would tell her what to do or where to go until it became obvious that no one was going to hold her hand. She lined up with the rest of the captains and tried to look professional.

Myrddin finished talking to one of the teachers and turned to address the room. "The shocks we're feeling are long-range attacks," Myrddin explained. "We still have some time before the bulk of the Dark One's forces arrive. At the moment, we're waiting for an update from our recon dragons."

The display on the projector changed, showing the terrain around the Nest more closely. "Based on the assaults so far, we're assuming that they're coming from the west and will be attacking that wing. It would be safe to assume they have some understanding of the setup of the Nest. We were unprepared during the last invasion, and I would not be surprised if they had done their homework."

Toppinir cleared his throat before speaking. "Do we have any guesses as to why they're attacking? It's been months since the meteor, and we've had no reports of any attention from the Dark One. What changed?"

An image of Vardis appeared on the projector screen. "As some of you might know," Myrddin explained, "two days ago, we retrieved a crashed ship from an unknown planet. The being inside, Vardis, stated that he was from the same dimension as the Dark One. I find the claim doubtful, but this sudden attack does lend credence to it. I have no doubt that the attack has to do with Vardis's arrival."

Alex was glad to hear that Myrddin didn't trust Vardis. It wasn't that the alien was lying, but how often did someone show up on your doorstep and offer to fix all your problems?

Roy, who was leaning against the wall chewing on his cigar, asked, "So, what's the plan? Are we going out to meet the Dark One's welcoming party, or are we waiting until they come here? I'd like to avoid what happened last time."

Myrddin's eyes softened as if he were experiencing the pain of the last invasion. "What happened before cannot and will not happen again," he said slowly. "Our defenses have been upgraded. No one can teleport into the Nest. We can keep the battle outside and protect the cadets who aren't combat-ready."

Roy seemed satisfied with the answer. Alex noticed that

the younger captains had yet to speak or ask any questions. They just stood and stared ahead, like the definition of good soldiers. Alex hoped she didn't look like them.

Myrddin spoke again. "We will be splitting into different groups. Roy, naturally, you're in charge of the mech riders. Toppinir, you and the rest of the faculty will lead seventy percent of the dragonrider captains. Alex, you will take Boundless and the remaining captains and their squads under your command."

Alex couldn't believe what Myrddin had said, and she furrowed her brow as she tried to understand his words. "Wait, what do you mean?"

Myrddin spoke sharply. "You will be leading your squad and at least twenty other riders. You've proven yourself in combat and leadership. Can you do this? I need to know now."

Alex looked at Roy, who slowly nodded.

Leading twenty riders? That meant that she'd be giving orders to some of the captains at her side, older and probably more combat seasoned veterans. *And I'm supposed to be responsible for them?* Alex asked herself.

But Alex was answering Myrddin before she even realized it. "Yeah, yeah, I can do it."

Myrddin smiled softly, a caring twinkle in his eye. "Good. I want you all in the air by the end of the hour. When intel on what we're up against comes in, I'll update all of your tactical planners. Dismissed."

The tone in the room changed, and the other captains relaxed. Myrddin left quickly, no doubt to implement whatever plans he had to set in motion.

Roy walked up behind Alex and clapped her on the shoulder, causing her to jump. "Why didn't you tell me he was going to do that?" Alex asked, hoping the sting could be heard in her voice.

"I didn't know," Roy answered curtly. "Myrddin plays a lot of stuff close to the chest. I'm proud of you for stepping up when you're needed. My suggestion is, don't get too chummy with anyone other than your team."

"Why would you say that?"

Roy sighed heavily. "There's no easy way to say this. People are going to die today, Alex. And you and I will be responsible for that."

In the back of Alex's mind, she had already known that. Hearing it from Roy didn't make it any easier to deal with, though. She clearly remembered the last invasion. Luckily, she had been able to save lives that day. But she knew that wasn't an option today. "Yeah, I kinda figured," Alex whispered.

"You know, if this is too much for you, I can talk to Myrddin. You and Boundless can be another squad. I don't want you cracking—"

"Under the pressure? You don't think I can do this?"

"It doesn't matter what I think you can do. It matters what you *know* you can do."

Alex thought about it again, without letting herself be as reactionary as she had been with Myrddin, but it didn't matter how many times she turned the question over in her head; there was no way to get around what was plainly in front of her. "I have to do this," she said. "And I think Myrddin knows that."

Roy squeezed Alex's shoulder, trying to bestow some encouragement on her. "Yeah, he usually does. Well, you heard the man. We gotta go."

Alex called each of her teammates and let them know what was going on. She didn't spend a whole lot of time talking, but she wanted to hear their voices. It was for that reason Roy had told her not to get too close to any of her squad. Alex already knew she wouldn't listen to that advice.

None of Boundless seemed even slightly worried that Alex was going to be leading such a large squad. They saw the choice as logical. Alex hadn't realized it until she hung up on Jollies, but she had been looking for affirmation. Even if she had said twice that she knew she could handle this, it still felt like too large a thing to get her head around.

Alex headed for the stables where Chine and the rest of her team's dragons were kept. She hadn't had a chance to speak to Chine since she'd been quarantined. Chine's telepathy was strong enough to reach through most of the Nest, but Alex hadn't heard from him this time. Maybe the Nest had expanded far enough that he couldn't reach her.

The stables were a vast room with steel walkways stretched over dragon dens, which were carved into the ground. The nests were different sizes so the dragons could rest comfortably. There was no ceiling, and the dragons were permitted to come and go as they pleased. A variety of tech sat on platforms on the walkways, most of it used to apply weapon augments to the dragons.

Chine poked his head up from his den when Alex walked into the stables. *I was starting to think you had forgotten about me.*

Alex leaped down into Chine's den. The floor was covered in the stones and precious jewels Chine had collected, and it was warm from his body heat. Alex leaned against the wall, resting her head against the steel. *They didn't tell you I was quarantined?*

They did, but I still worry. I'm glad you were finally released.

I'm assuming they told you about the invasion.

Chine nodded as he exhaled a small cloud of smoke. *Yes,*

we've been told. It is good you made it down here before the rest of the riders. You seem to be troubled by something.

Alex moved away from the wall and lay down on the stones. An emerald caught her eye, and she was reminded of the green streak from the meteor. *Yeah, but when am I not?* She sighed. *They made me a captain today, I guess. I'm in charge of a squad, not just Boundless this time.*

Are you afraid you aren't capable of leading them well?

Not quite. I know I can lead. That's become pretty apparent. And I'm never worried about Boundless, you know. They can all take care of themselves. There's a reason why we've been pushed so hard. We can handle it.

Chine's face was usually unreadable since his reptilian features didn't leave much room for expression. But sometimes, Chine's eyes looked almost caring. *Then what are you worried about?*

Alex looked unhappy. *People are going to die. There's no getting around it. My command is going to kill someone. An order that I give will be the cause of someone's death.*

Dustling, you will not be the cause. The Dark One is the cause. You aren't sending anyone to their death. The Dark One is the one robbing mortals of their lives, not you.

Alex knew he was right, but it didn't make her feel any less terrible or responsible. *Yeah, I guess you're right.* She stood up. *Roy made it sound like it was something I have to deal with.*

The dragon shook his head as he stretched his wings over Alex. *If that is what Roy thinks, he is wrong. Your heart is large. You care for people even when you don't realize you do. That is a strength, not a weakness.*

Alex chuckled. *You think so?*

Now you're fishing for compliments.

Alex threw her arms up and laughed as she walked away. *All right, all right! Sometimes I want to be told how great I am. Sue me.*

An explosion shook the Nest, and Alex's smile fell from her face. "We better start getting ready," she said aloud. "It's time to sling the heavy stuff on."

Chine groaned as he stretched his legs, standing to his full height as Alex leaped out of the den and went over to the augment platform. She scrolled through her options, trying to think of what would be useful for enemies she knew nothing about. Then she remembered what had happened when she had been separated from him during the fight to get to the ship. *Hey, I wanted to ask you something.*

The dragon poked his head out of the den. *What would you like to know?*

When our link was broken, something happened when I was fighting that giant. I got a sudden surge of power and burst into flames briefly. It was like when I activate my anchor power, but the anchor was dead. What do you think that was?"

Chine scratched his chin against the rim of the den. *Hm. Your anchor power merely helps you process draconic fluid into your body and metabolize it. Perhaps, your body is getting better at doing the processing. You might not need the anchor eventually.*

Alex glanced down at her dragon anchor, running her robotic hand across it. *Huh. That's kinda cool. All right, Chine, let's get you suited up.*

CHAPTER SIX

Team Boundless assembled in the stables not long after Alex had finished fitting Chine with the augments she thought would be best. There was a very somber mood amongst them since the last invasion was still fresh in everyone's mind. That was what Alex assumed, at least. She couldn't have been the only one to have been deeply affected by that day.

Each member of the team went to their dragon's platform and started to look through the options of augments to load up with. There weren't any jokes, and everyone looked very serious. The only person from Boundless who wasn't there was Jim. He must be with the other mech riders, Alex thought.

Alex commed Jim and asked him whether he was going to be rolling out with her or the mech riders. He let her know he was still riding with Boundless, but he had to take care of a couple of technical issues with his mech before launching. There was no way he was heading into a fight without knowing his mech was running at its best.

After Alex hung up on Jim, Gill walked up behind her. Alex had no idea how long he'd been standing there. It could have been for the whole conversation. "Jeez, you scared the crap out of me."

Gill walked out of the shadows and around Alex so she could see him better. "I'm sorry," he said softly. "I didn't mean to alarm you. I wanted to ask you how you were holding up."

Alex looked around to give herself time to think. She didn't want to have a heart to heart at the moment, but she knew Gill wasn't going to let it go. He never did once he got something set in his mind. "I've been better. Could be worse, but it could also be less terrible, you know."

"The last time we fought off the Dark One's army here, we were unprepared. This time it's different, but it feels the same."

"Yeah, I know what you mean. Just like that day. My guts are all messed up. At least before, we had the benefit of being surprised. It was all adrenaline. I felt like I was operating on autopilot the entire time."

"Not like today. We've been through worse than this, but it feels like it's the first few weeks of classes. I'm glad we'll be able to make up for the first attack today."

Alex hadn't thought of it like that. It was almost like they were being given a second chance, and this time, they were prepared for what was coming for them. All the lives that hung in the balance were going to be protected. That was what mattered.

Gill drifted away silently as he often did, leaving Alex alone with her thoughts. Instead of dwelling on them, Alex walked over to Brath and took a seat next to his platform.

Brath's dragon Furi was the largest of all the dragons at

the Nest. A hulking red beast, he was the only creature at the Nest with a quicker temper than Brath.

The gnome was sitting on Furi's back, fiddling with the anchor component attached to the dragon's spine. He looked up from his work as Alex approached. "What's up?"

Alex checked Furi's augments. "You find anything you want to use?"

Brath pointed to the dragon's right shoulder, which had a large plasma cannon attached to it. "Saw this a couple of days ago," Brath said. "Supposed to be twice as strong as the smaller cannons, and I think Furi is the only one big enough to use it. Can't think of a better chance to test it."

"Comfortable being part of a larger squad?"

Brath looked annoyed at the new line of questioning. Talking about weapons was more his style. Getting to the root of how he felt wasn't something Alex thought she was going to be able to do with one conversation, but she wanted him to know that she cared enough to try.

"As long as they don't get in my way, it'll be all right," the gnome said. "Don't make me hold back because you don't want me showing up the new guys."

"Wouldn't dream of it, Brath. Let me know if you need anything before we head out."

"Gotcha, boss."

It was still unbelievable to Alex that she and Brath were on speaking terms now. When she'd first arrived at the Nest, Brath had devoted the majority of his time to making sure Alex felt as alone and pathetic as possible. All that had changed the day of the invasion, when Brath had seen what Alex was really made of. In a lot of ways, that was when Alex had found that out too.

Alex made her way over to Jollies, who was attending to her dragon, Amber. Jollies was still in the process of choosing her augments. It always took her noticeably longer than the rest of the riders, but the pixie found the most specific and interesting augments. Her loadouts were generally the envy of every other rider. "Yo, Jollies!" Alex shouted.

She turned at the sound of her name. Her eyes were glistening with tears, and she hiccupped slightly as her lips trembled.

Alex rushed over to her, and the pixie floated into Alex's hands. "Oh, my God, Jollies, are you okay?" Alex asked.

Jollies' voice was small, hardly above a whisper. "I don't know why I'm scared, Alex, but I am. I'm so scared."

Alex didn't know what to say. That was what she felt as well. She had no idea where the fear was coming from, why it cropped up so fast, or where it had been hiding during the last few months, incubating and growing stronger. It was here now, and if it was here for her, it must have been there for the rest of the team too.

Alex held her hand up to her face so she could look her friend in the eye. "Hey, it's going to be okay," she said. "We're not scared kids anymore. You got that? We're dragonriders now.

Jollies nodded as she wiped away her tears. "Yeah, I know," she said. "Still feels like I'm a scared kid, though."

"Same here."

Jollies laughed as she floated back over to Amber. "Don't worry. I'll pull it together."

Alex walked to Chine's platform and hopped up. She watched Chine curling and uncurling his tail. Even the dragon was nervous about the upcoming battle.

A beep went off on Alex's dragon anchor. It was an incoming call from Abby. Alex opened the message and the anchor projected a holograph of Abby in front of her. "Whoa, that's new," Alex yelped.

Abby smiled widely as she fist-pumped. "Sweet, it worked," she exclaimed. "Been trying to get the new software upgrades to you guys for a bit. Anyway, I took a look at that rod for y'all. Got bad news for ya."

Alex groaned as she braced herself for whatever Abby was going to say. "This isn't one of those good news/bad news situations, is it?"

"Nah. All bad news. That thing is dangerous. Severs the connection between your dragon and anchor and blocks all telepathic communication. And here's the doozy: it stays active until someone kills the person who used it."

"That's great. I was starting to get my hopes up about this mission."

Abby's next smile was not nearly as enthusiastic. "Yeah, don't shoot the messenger, okay? But don't worry, I ain't gonna leave y'all hanging. I'm working on something. Kinda like a firewall."

"Are you going to have it finished in the next ten minutes?"

"Uh, no. In a rush or something?"

Alex nervously chuckled. "Kinda in the middle of an invasion."

"Oh, well, hope you don't have a lot of these. Good luck! I should let y'all get to it."

Alex couldn't help laughing at how matter of fact Abby was about all of this. Even though she was the same age as Alex and the rest of the riders, Abby seemed to be acclimating to working with Myrddin and Middang3ard. "Yeah, yeah," Alex said. "Hey, if I survive, we should, like, hang out."

"Ugh. Agreed. You have no idea how weird it is working with people in their three thousandth year of life. Y'all go wreck them."

Alex hung up the comm and jumped on top of Chine. She pulled up the tactical display and checked to see if there were any more updates to the current situation.

The intel had come in, and the display showed the terrain

around the Nest. The area was filled with red dots denoting enemies. There was also a message attached to the display. Alex clicked on it.

Alex's ears were overwhelmed by frantic screaming, someone begging for their life, repeating over and over that they didn't want to die. Alex turned off the message as fast as she could. She climbed off and sat down next to Chine and tried to control her breathing.

Alex's comm rang, and she looked down to see a message from Myrddin. It was time to go.

The dragonriders gathered in the main hall, where the massacre had taken place a few months ago. Alex thought it must be Myrddin's intention to face what everyone was thinking rather than running away from it.

Alex appreciated the notion. She knew it was still on her team's mind, and there was no way the rest of the riders had forgotten about the atrocities that had taken place here.

The captains stood on the main stage behind Myrddin, who was behind the podium facing the cadets. The dragonriders were lined up in rows facing the stage, their red and black uniforms shining brightly.

The mech riders, a smaller corps, stood to the left of the dragonriders. They wore blue uniforms with an insignia and a phrase written in Elvish that Alex had meant to ask Gill about.

The dragon and mech riders stood silently watching the stage as another explosion rocked the Nest. You wouldn't have been able to tell by looking at Myrddin. His face didn't show any sign of interest in the dangers that lay beyond the Nest.

Myrddin stepped closer to the podium and cupped his

hands together, resting them on his stomach. "Today, the Dark One has dared to come to our doors once more," Myrddin said. "Today, we gather in this hall where so many passed, and we remember them. The dead did not sacrifice their lives for us. We must be honest with ourselves. Their lives were stolen."

Alex looked at the teachers and the other captains out of the corner of her eye as Myrddin continued speaking. "But today is a new day, and we are wiser and stronger than before. Today is the day that we avenge our fallen brothers and sisters. Today is the day the Dark One will be reminded that the Wasp's Nest is a place of warriors. Fight well."

Myrddin stepped away from the podium as Roy took his place. "You have your assignments already, so you know who you're teaming up with. The game plan is simple—we're going to meet them head-on and fight them off. That being said, keep your ears out for comms and individual orders and formations from your captains. There's no way to get around this; some of us aren't coming back. You sure as hell better make sure you give as good as we get. Dismissed."

Alex followed the rest of the captains as they left the podium. This was it.

The sky filled with dragons and mechs as the riders departed the Nest, rising into the clouds. There were hundreds of them, different breeds and colors. Alex could never have imagined anything like it. There was no way the Dark One was going to win this battle.

Roy, Toppinir, Alex, and the rest of the captains were at the front of the horde of dragons, their respective squads behind them. Alex checked her dragon anchor as she leaned forward and scratched Chine behind his horns.

A comm came through from Roy. "Dragonriders, we got a nice bit of intel. The Dark One's got some new doohickey that'll kill your connection to your dragons. There's nothing we can do about that since we haven't had enough time to figure out how to stop that, but there's a system in place, thanks to some friends over at Earth's HQ. If you get disconnected, your anchor will send out a signal to the closest mech to come scoop you out of the sky. Think about it as getting a free sky-diving lesson."

There were chuckles across the open comm channel. Alex was glad Roy knew how to defuse a stressful situation. She felt like there were worse things than plummeting to the ground after being knocked off Chine.

There was no fanfare at the beginning of the attack. Roy simply rocketed forward, Toppinir following him, and Alex took that as a sign to get moving. The dragon army headed to the coordinates that had been provided.

There were a few miles out from the Nest when Roy stopped.

They had arrived at the coordinates, but there was nothing there. That couldn't be right, Alex thought as she checked her tactical display. The coordinates were correct. The Dark One's army was supposed to be right in front of them.

Roy opened his cockpit and lit his cigar. "Hm," he murmured. "This is a little anticlimactic."

Alex focused on the ground below them. They weren't too high up, and her dragon eyes could pick up the smallest detail. What caught her eye was an odd shimmer, something like a ripple across still water. "There's something down there," she announced.

Suddenly, there was a loud whirring sound like that of a power generator turning on. It grew louder and louder until a blast of plasma nearly the size of a red dragon came shooting up from the ground. "Incoming!" Alex shouted.

The riders scattered, Alex veering hard to the left to avoid the attack. The plasma blast soared through the air, suddenly exploding and sending smaller bolts at the riders, who dove toward the source of the attack.

Alex's eyes focused again on the shimmer beneath her, and she saw something moving. "Roy, I'm going down there," she shouted.

Roy hooted loudly as he got back into his mech. He plummeted toward the shimmer with a mad cackle as he threw his thrusters into afterburn. Alex and the rest of the riders were right behind him.

lex, Roy, and the rest of the dragonriders passed through the shimmering veil. Once through, Alex pulled up on her dragon anchor, causing Chine to stop and fly backward a little bit. She was not the only one to do that.

The Dark One's forces were coming over the hill. The army was led by what appeared to be slugs nearly the size of houses. Their bodies were pale blue, and they had eyes all over. Electrodes and electronic components covered their soft flesh. An orc sat atop each, its body from the waist down melded into the slugs through some obscene mixture of technology and flesh.

Plasma cannons half as large as the slug's bodies were strapped to each creature's back. That must have been where the whirring had come from.

Behind the slugs were creatures that Alex could never have imagined. They were taller than the slugs, with long spindly legs, stretched and spider-like. Their heads looked like ancient, rotting human heads with long stringy hair hanging from their gaunt faces. Their skin was covered in steel plates, and they lumbered along like ghosts caught in a dream.

Roy's voice came through the comm. "What the hell are those? You ever see anything like that before?"

Toppinir replied, "No."

"This is an attack by the Dark One, right? 'Cause this does not fit his M.O."

Alex pointed to the orc/slug fusion creatures and narrowed her eyes to get a better look at the tech that connected the orcs to the slugs. She could see there were multiple orcs embedded in the skin of the slugs, some of them barely visible, others merely a hand forcing its way through the slug's skin.

"That's the Dark One's tech. I've seen it in some of the briefings. Stuff like that's been cropping up throughout Middang3ard."

"You're right," Roy agreed. "Well, we got our work cut out for us. Let's get started. Charge!"

Roy blasted forward, and Alex took off after him. "Boundless," Alex called, "I want you as close to me as possible. Jollies, take point. Get as close to those things as you can, but don't engage. I want to get an idea of what we're up against."

Jollies and Amber zoomed to the front of the charging army, easily flying faster than the other riders and the mechs. "On it," the pixie called.

"Brath, I want you in the front with me. Gill, get behind us, and Jim, link up with the rest of the mech riders. Squad A, we're going in slow. We don't know what these things have ready for us, other than those anchor detachers, so be ready."

The whirring of the slug's plasma cannons began anew. The sound was louder and more oppressive up close. They were gearing up to launch an attack.

Alex looked around to see what else was down there. So far, she didn't see any aerial fighters. Maybe the Dark One's plan was to ground all the riders, turn this into a ground fight, and see what happened. Alex didn't know why, though. The last ground fight, the dragonriders had won.

Jollies' shrill voice squeaked over the comm, "You're not going to believe this until you see it. Heading back to the main group."

As if the Dark One's forces had heard her, a change came over the slugs. They stopped their forward movement and began to shake and convulse. The orc bodies inside the sagging flesh of the slugs forced their way through the skin.

As the orcs climbed out of the slugs, spewing bright blue fluid everywhere, they screeched loudly, techno-organic wings sprouting from their backs. The wings were razor-sharp, and the orcs had cannons mounted on their backs.

The orcs stood, steam rising from their bodies, then spread their wings and took off, heading straight for the dragonriders.

The slugs fired their cannons, sending the plasma blasts into the thick of the riders, who took evasive action, then spread out, preparing for the inevitable explosion of the plasma blast.

The orcs didn't seem to care about the plasma bolts and kept flying toward the riders, slashing at them with their metallic wings.

Alex pulled up, drawing her scythe from her dragon anchor and watching closely to see if any of the orcs near her were holding black rods. She couldn't see any, but they were moving fast.

An orc flew past Alex, slashing at her with its wings. Alex ducked in time, avoiding having the razor edges slice through her neck. She raised her scythe and caught the orc in the chest, which nearly yanked her off her dragon. Luckily, she was still anchored.

The sky had turned into a scene of chaos. There were hundreds of the flying orcs aggressively attacking the dragonriders as if they had no fear for their lives. Alex could see a dull green light glowing in their eyes as if their brains had been hollowed out and replaced with something else.

Below, the lanky spider creatures with the faces of men opened their mouths. Black drool and gunk fell out as they regurgitated giant chunks of black rock, stretching it out in the shape of a rod. "Those are it!" Alex shouted. "The spiders have the rods!"

Roy flew to the front lines as he shouted, "Mech riders to the front! We need to take down those spiders!"

The mechs detached from the main group of riders and headed for the spider monsters, weaving between the orcs. The winged creatures tried to attach themselves to the mechs and rip them open with their wings and plasma axes.

The sheer number of orcs looked overwhelming. Alex wasn't certain if the mech riders were going to be able to make it to the spiders without being ripped out of their mechs. They would need backup. "Boundless, we're backing up the mechs. Squad A, try to keep the orcs off of us, but don't get too close to the spiders. Stay as far back as you can. We don't know the range of those rods."

Gill, Brath, and Jollies flew closer to Alex, and they pushed forward, Chine and Furi lit the sky with their fire as Alex hacked at any orc foolish enough to get close to her.

Roy dropped on the closest spider creature, floating in front of its grotesque face. He opened fire with everything that he had, unloading his machine gun and missiles onto the black rod.

The spider creature screeched in pain as it reared up on its hind legs. A shock wave erupted from the black rod.

Alex could see the energy signature of the shockwave. She pulled up on the anchor, avoiding the wave. "Chine, you can see that, right?"

The dragon banked to the right to avoid an orc, blasting it with a flame attack. "Yes, but I'm not sure the rest of the dragons can see the same frequencies we can."

"Link up with them telepathically. Watch the shockwaves and let them know when they're coming. I'll take care of any orcs that get too close. We're gonna keep moving forward."

"Understood."

Alex drove Chine toward the closest spider creature. Jim had joined Roy, and they were working on destroying the black rods. They had the firepower, but it was slow work, almost like mining an ore deposit. Alex wondered how her weapons were going to fare against the rods.

Brath flew to Alex's side, and the two of them headed for the same creature as orcs flew past them, Alex cutting down anything that got too close to her. They made it to the spider and flew past it, firing their flame attacks at the rod.

The heat from the flames cracked the rod. It didn't fall or shatter, but it was damaged. Then it began to hum and vibrate loudly. "Pull back!" Alex shouted as she yanked up on her dragon anchor.

Chine and Furi soared upward, away from the erupting shockwave. Alex watched it spread toward the dragonriders dealing with the bulk of the winged orcs. The rods had an extremely long range, apparently, and the shockwave was going to hit them. "Roy, the wave is coming for our riders!" Alex shouted over the comm.

Roy and Jim disengaged from the creature they were fighting and headed back toward the others as Jim shouted, "We're on it!"

Alex and Brath flew back down toward the rod, firing everything they had at the head of the spider creature. It reeled back in pain, a muffled scream ushering from its mouth.

Chine fired another flame attack at the rod as Brath guided Furi around, flying a good distance away and then charging full force at the black rod, tackling it with all the force the red dragon could muster.

The rod split down the middle, separating from the spider creature's mouth. It fell and crushed one of the slugs making its way toward the Nest.

Alex flew in closer to the slug's head and slammed her scythe down in between its eyes. The creature screeched in pain and threw back its head, toppling into the spider creature at its side. Both of them crashing to the ground in a heap of thin, kicking legs.

Alex shouted, "Squad A, how are you holding up?"

One of the squad members replied, "We're holding our own. The orcs are vicious, but they seem to mostly be a distraction. The slugs on the ground have all the firepower, but we can't get to them with the rods still active."

"I want you to divert your attention to the slugs. Ignore the orcs as best as you can. We need to take care of their artillery."

"Roger!"

Alex banked left, flying back toward the remaining spider creatures. "Boundless, the priority is the rods. Anything you can do to bring them down, do it!"

Out of the corner of Alex's eye, she could see Jollies charging forward, electricity sparking off Amber as they headed for the nearest spider. Gill was right behind her, Timber firing plasma missiles from his shoulders.

The plasma cannons connected with the rod hanging from the creature's mouth and Jollies flew around it. Lightning jumped from Amber's scales, sending a chain-lightning attack up the creature's body.

Alex and Chine headed for the same spider creature, the dragon shooting ether flames at the rod and Alex swinging her scythe with all the force of her robotic arm as they flew by.

The black rod cracked and Brath repeated his earlier strategy and slammed into it, cracking it even farther down the middle.

The spider creature shrieked in pain as it stumbled back, but before the crystal broke away, a shockwave erupted from it.

Alex was able to dodge the shockwave, as was Brath. The wave hit Jollies and Gill.

Jollies detached from Amber, but the two were so small that Jollies managed to grab her dragon before they got too far apart, holding tightly to his horns to keep from falling off.

Gill, on the other hand, was not so lucky. The wave hit him and Timber hard, sending the drow flying through the air as a swarm of orcs headed for him.

Alex sent Chine rocketing toward him. They cut through the orcs who were fighting to get to Gill. Alex reached out, trying to grasp Gill's hand.

An orc sideswiped Alex from the left, hitting her with its wings, and cutting her across the chest with enough force to detach her from Chine. She went flying through the air, reaching for the dragon's wings but narrowly missing them. She plummeted toward the earth.

Both Alex and Gill were in freefall. Gill pulled his plasma pistol from his holster, firing at every orc that flew at him with the coolness of someone walking down the street to their favorite store.

Alex still gripped her scythe in one hand, the other putting pressure on the wound across her chest. She was losing blood, and she wasn't sure how fast. The pain was hardly noticeable since her body was flooded with adrenaline. All she could think about was keeping the orcs flying at her from getting too close.

Jim and Roy turned away from the orcs in front of them and flew after the falling riders. Alex saw them approaching, but her vision was beginning to blur. A group of orcs headed for her, and it looked as if they would get there before either Roy or Jim.

Alex grabbed Gill's arm and pulled him closer to her. As they hurtled toward the ground, Gill continued to unload shot after shot at anything getting close to them. He picked off the orcs that Alex had been worried would arrive before the mech riders did.

Roy swooped under Gill, opening his cockpit and allowing Gill to fall gently into it. Jim executed the same maneuver beneath Alex.

He reached out to her, trying to grab her hand and pull her into the cockpit.

As Alex's fingers wrapped around Jim's hand, an orc hit her from the left and she was knocked away from Jim. Its wings slashed her arm, and she lost her grip on her scythe.

Jim hit his thrusters and attempted to get closer to Alex, but a group of orcs flocked to him, covering his mech.

Alex hit her comm and shouted, "Squad A! Report!"

A couple of voices came through at the same time, but Alex heard one louder than the other. "We've taken out all of the spiders, and the orcs are retreating! The slugs have stopped moving forward."

"Retreat! Head back to the Nest to regroup and finish them off."

"Roger!"

The ground was coming for Alex. She was going to hit hard, and that would be the end. There was something oddly comforting about knowing death would be swift.

An orc flew toward Alex with its wings outstretched,

hoping to slash her. Alex saw her opening, and as the orc got closer, she grabbed its throat and swung around behind it. She locked her robotic arm around the orc's neck and steered it to the ground.

Alex hit the earth with immense speed, the orc taking the bulk of the impact. When she stumbled to her feet, she noticed the ground was soft and squishy. "What the hell?" she muttered to herself.

Suddenly, the ground grew unstable, and Alex fell forward. She wasn't on the ground, she was on the back of one of the slugs. "Chine!" she called. "I'm down here!"

Alex didn't know if the dragon could hear her. There was no reply as she looked at the slug's foul body, more orc hands and heads trying to force themselves out of the putrid flesh.

The presence of Alex had awakened something within the orcs. Those who had been docile under the skin were now moaning loudly and trying to pull themselves out.

Alex backed away, not knowing where to go. She tried to pull her scythe from her dragon anchor, but nothing happened. A shockwave from one of the black rods must have hit her. She was defenseless.

The orcs continued to claw their way out of the slug. *This is it*, Alex thought. *I did my best, and that was all I could do.*

Rage was the only word for what Alex felt. To know her life was about to end in such a fashion pulled at something deep within her that she did not know existed. Her veins began to burn, as well as her eyes.

The air around Alex grew hot and flames erupted, covering her body as energy radiated from it.

The pillar of flames she generated stretched skyward, engulfing everything above and around her. The fire seared through the flesh of the slugs and the orcs who clawed their way toward her, reducing them all to ash.

Alex fell through the miasma of charred bodies. As her

eyes began to flutter closed, her body became weightless. *What's happening?* she wondered hazily.

Her dragon's voice in her head comforted her. *I am here for you, Dustling,* he said before everything went black.

CHAPTER EIGHT

Alex stood in a room which was all white. There was no furniture. The walls did not seem to be walls. She was ankle-deep in water, and she had both her arms. Someone was singing, but she did not recognize the song or the voice.

Vardis crouched across from her, staring into the water. He looked over his shoulder. "Oh," he said, "you're finally here."

When Alex spoke, it was not with her mouth, and it was not telepathy as she experienced it with Chine. This was something else. It was a flurry of emotions and concepts that crystalized in what could pass for language in such a place. She had felt this aboard the meteor.

Where is here?

Vardis stood, flicked water off of his fingers, and walked over to Alex. *This is your mind,* he explained. *Or something like it. You're sleeping now, much like when we first spoke. The only difference is that this is not a natural sleep. I'm assuming you passed out during the battle.*

Alex looked down at her hands. They were quivering,

bending in and out of the light as if they weren't real. *How are you able to do this?*

We are linked. When I first saw you, I connected with you telepathically as a failsafe in case something happened to me. I wasn't certain I could trust any of you yet. Not the most prudent of means to ensure my safety, but it was the best I could do.

Alex crouched next to the water. There were minnows swimming under the surface. *Why didn't you think you could trust us?* she asked. *Wasn't that the reason you came here to meet with us?*

Vardis knelt beside Alex. *I traveled here to deliver a weapon to destroy the Dark One. I wasn't sure who or what I was going to find. For all I knew, you people could have been pawns of the Dark One. There are enough in this realm to have made that a possibility.*

You came from the place the Dark One is from, didn't you?

For the first time, Alex saw something like emotion in the alien's eyes. Its eyes conveyed a deep sense of loss, perhaps more than Alex believed anyone was capable of feeling. *I came from a place the Dark One intimately touched. I do not know where he came from, only where he has been.*

The white room contorted, its edges blurring and stretching as the light disappeared and was replaced by the darkness of space, stars birthing themselves as the universe stretched out around them. *This was my home,* Vardis said.

The view zoomed in on one planet that did not look much different than Earth. They continued to get closer, passing through the atmosphere and the clouds until they were on the land, watching other members of Vardis's race going about their lives in a city that nearly reached the stars.

The Dark One came to our planet in silence. Much like what has happened here, he infected our people through means we did not understand. Now we know it to be some kind of mind-controlling technology, but we did not then. Agents of the Dark One walked amongst us, and we were ignorant of it. Slowly, a war brewed.

The cities crumbled to dust and were carried away by the wind. Members of Vardis' race fought each other. Bodies littered the ground, the dead stacked in piles. A pale white child wearing a buck's head mask walked amongst the corpses.

Vardis spoke again. *We were unprepared for the war. It did not take long before our planet was ravaged, our people destroyed or scattered. There were resistances, but how were we to fight against ourselves? Our world was soon destroyed. Those he was not able to enslave were killed.*

Now there were images of mines, of an alien race burrowing into the ground. There was something deep and strange down there. Alex didn't know how she knew, but she was certain that whatever was there should not be disturbed.

When Vardis spoke, the mines disappeared, replaced by what looked like an oversized child, something swollen with loose skin, crying and screaming. *The Dark One began to dig deep into our planet. No one knew why. The Resistance couldn't figure it out. He seemed unconcerned with minerals or ore, but he continued to dig.*

The two were standing above the planet, which was graying. Alex could see the vegetation dying and fading. The seas were drying up. *I do not know how, but the Dark One began to devour our world. He sucked it dry of all life. After a while, it started to affect more than our home.*

Vardis and others like him were walking in long lines in an endless desert. Their bodies were gaunt, their bones prominent. Many had fallen to the wayside on the endless march, their skin turning to ash and floating off into the bloodred sky. *We were dying, and the planet was drained.*

The planet grew red amongst the stars. Fires erupted across it as the seas boiled and evaporated. The core sizzled and bloomed as the earth cracked and flames erupted from its bowels. Then the planet exploded, sending its remains into space.

The room was white again, and only Alex and Vardis remained. *What are you doing here?*

As I said before, I discovered a weapon to destroy the Dark One. I wish to give it to you in the hope that this war can finally be brought to an end.

Great! Where is it? If you have something to stop the Dark One, let's do it.

Vardis shook his head slowly, his eyes filled with sadness. *It is not here. I had to hide it from the Dark One. It is on a moon in the realm you are from—Earth's moon. And you are the only one who can get it.*

Alex scowled and folded her arms. *Are you serious? Why can't Myrddin? I'm just a kid. A soldier. There are—*

Because I trust you. That is why.

CHAPTER NINE

Alex snapped awake, jerking backward, scrambling and trying to get away from whatever was around her. Hands grabbed her and she reached for her scythe, uncertain of where the enemy was until she heard a familiar voice squeak, "Alex, it's okay!"

The adrenaline began to drain from Alex's body when she recognized Jollies' voice. Her vision started to return.

Team Boundless and Roy surrounded Alex. She looked around, trying to figure out where she was. It was somewhere near the Nest, but they weren't inside. "Where are we?" she asked.

Roy and Jim helped her to her feet. They were in the outer section of the Nest in an alcove that overlooked the valley. The rest of the captains and the mech and dragonriders were spread out around the alcove. The riders' dragons floated above.

Alex walked over to the edge and looked over. "What are we doing up here?"

Roy stood beside Alex and lit his cigar. "Someone was

smart enough to give their squad the call to retreat," he said. "It was a good one. Looked like we were winning the damn thing. Turned out, that's not exactly what was happening."

Roy pointed into the distance. The techno-organic slugs were still making their way toward the Nest, a black swarm of orcs above them.

Alex sighed and leaned her head back in frustration. "Are you kidding me? I thought we killed most of those damn things."

"Language, Alex."

"I can fight for Middang3ard, but I can't use a PG curse word? So, who's going to fill me in on what the hell is happening?"

Roy knocked his cigar's ashes over the edge of the alcove. "Like I said, we retreated. Myrddin thought it was a good idea. Said he was going to come out here and meet us. Doesn't seem like Myrddin's style to sit back and wait for his favorite facility to be overrun."

Alex looked around, trying to find Myrddin. "Where is he?"

The double doors of the Nest opened, and Myrddin walked into the alcove. He didn't bother to stop and address anyone as he breezed past and peered at the valley.

He held a thin white wand in his hand and raised it above his head. Energy crackled around him as he floated into the air, his eyes turning bright white, lightning flashing from them and surrounding the rest of his body.

The old wizard began speaking softly under his breath and drawing sigils in the air, his wand moving elegantly as he traced the elaborate shapes. His voice grew louder and louder until it sounded as if it were a force of nature.

Dark clouds spread through the sky. A storm was coming, and it was obvious Myrddin was the one who was weaving it. Thunder crackled in the distance.

Roy leaned against his mech as the rest of the riders and captains moved in to get a better view of what was happening. "Oh." He chuckled. "You guys have never seen Myrddin in action before. This will be a treat."

Myrddin pointed his wand in the direction of the Dark One's forces. His voice echoed throughout the valley as he spoke a dead language, one lost long before humanity arose.

The sky ripped open and bolts of lightning the size of city blocks tore through the air, striking the slugs as they traveled through the valley. When the bolts struck the ground, flames erupted.

As the flames licked at the slugs, winds swirled around, pulling the flames and the slugs into a vortex of lightning and fire. The flaming tornados danced, leaving destruction in their wake.

Above, the old wizard vibrated with energy. A pulse of fire rushed from his body, sending all the riders flying backward as Myrddin gave a cry that sounded as if it had been ripped from a god.

In the distance, the flaming tornados converged, transforming into a larger tornado that stretched to the sky. Another massive bolt of lightning struck the eye of the tornado and a flash of light spread through the valley, bright enough that it could have been the sun. It momentarily blinded everyone.

When Alex could see again, the valley was empty. There was no grass, no trees—nothing.

Myrddin floated back down to the ground and waved his wand one more time. A shimmering bubble spread over the Nest, stretching out as far as the path of destruction.

The wizard walked over to Alex, his movements labored and looking painful. He was breathing very deeply, and his eyes looked extremely tired. "Alex, we need to speak. There are more reinforcements coming since this will only hold for so long. I need to know what Vardis told you."

Alex was surprised Myrddin knew she'd had a dream about Vardis. "How did you know about that?"

"That is not what's important. What you were told is."

CHAPTER TEN

Myrddin and Alex met in the wizard's study. No one else was allowed in. When he stepped into the room, he went straight to a chair and collapsed in it. He looked tired but not defeated, and his eyes were still bright with life. "When you were unconscious," he started. "Vardis spoke to you, didn't he?"

Alex took a seat next to Myrddin as she tried to recollect what Vardis had told her. "He said we were telepathically linked."

"Yes, I know you two are linked. That is one of the troubling aspects of all this. Did he say why he linked to you?"

"Because he trusted me."

Myrddin leaned forward as he stared at Alex. His eyes were impossible to read. Alex knew he was thinking, but she couldn't tell what. "That is disconcerting," he muttered.

Alex felt her pride flash as her cheeks burned red. "Why is that disconcerting?"

Myrddin's face softened as he reached over to his coffee table and picked up a glass of water that appeared on it. "Please do not take offense, Alex, but you are a child. If there was a matter of this importance, Vardis should have spoken with me. That is what is disconcerting."

Only a child? Fighting in a war, leading an entire squad, risking my life? And I'm just a child?

Silence hung in the air between Alex and Myrddin as they watched each other. Alex couldn't believe that was how Myrddin thought of her. After all of the work she'd done for him, after everything she'd sacrificed and experienced, Myrddin didn't think she was anything other than a kid.

Myrddin didn't seem to care about how Alex was reacting to his opinion. "What did he tell you?"

Alex thought Myrddin could ask Vardis himself if he was so certain of how important he was, but she also knew this wasn't the time or place for such pettiness. However hurt her feelings were, it wasn't going to help the situation. She had intel, and the war effort needed it. "He said he hid the weapon on Earth's moon."

Myrddin clicked his tongue, folded his hands, and sat quietly for a bit. "Interesting." Then he rose and walked to his desk. "Alex, your leadership skills saved many lives today. You were the only one wise enough to do what they all knew they should have done. I commend you."

Myrddin rested his hand on his desk, leaning over it. He looked immensely old. "That is why I tell you this in complete honesty. I do not know what to think of Vardis. I can't figure him out, and that is dangerous. Do you understand what I'm saying?"

Alex didn't. She'd never seen Myrddin speak so candidly, and it was upsetting. "I'm sorry. I'm sorry, sir, but I don't follow."

"Ignorance is dangerous. It ends in wars, and in this situation, we are ignorant."

"What am I supposed to do?"

Myrddin turned to face Alex, his face tired and worn. "I don't know," he admitted. "I just don't know."

Team Boundless had gathered in the stables to prepare for their next mission. Myrddin and Alex had sent out a briefing to let them know they were going to be traveling to Earth. There was a weapon on Earth's moon that had to be retrieved.

The members of Boundless were beyond excited to visit Alex's realm. They were joking and talking about it loudly as they prepared their dragons for the trip.

Alex watched them from afar. She was excited to go home, but her conversation with Myrddin had left her anxious. The wizard was running all this. To see him at a loss for what to do or think worried her. On top of that, they still weren't certain when the Dark One's reinforcements would arrive. Myrddin might be sending Boundless to Earth in the middle of a siege.

In any other situation, Alex would have been ecstatic to go back to Earth, even if it was for a mission. Something felt off about this, though. She didn't know why she shouldn't trust Vardis, other than Myrddin's mistrust.

Jim noticed Alex standing on the upper level, looking down at the rest of the team. "Hey, you going to join us anytime soon?" he called, "We're going home, dude!"

Alex jumped down and walked over to him. "Yeah, I know," she said, "I'm super excited."

Jollies fluttered over to Alex, gushing, "I can't wait to see what your realm is like! I've never seen a lot of humans up close."

Brath groaned as he dragged the augments he had removed off Furi. "Why would you want to see a bunch of humans? Just imagine Alex and Jim and think about more of them. Though I doubt they'll be as—you know, what, never mind."

Gill grabbed Brath's beard as the gnome walked by. "Were you about to compliment Jim and Alex?" he asked.

Brath slapped Gill's hand away. "Not even. I was going to say the humans will probably be more annoying than Alex and Jim. Damn. And I've told you before, don't grab my beard. It takes a lot of time to get it looking this good."

Gill and Jim cracked up as they watched Brath hobble off, huffing and puffing and muttering under his breath. When Jim saw that Alex wasn't laughing, he came up to her and took her hand. "You okay?"

Alex squeezed Jim's hand, but she was aware she was doing it more for Jim than herself. "Yeah, everything's cool. Can't wait to take you guys to my favorite pizza spot."

Before Alex could say anything else, the comm interrupted her. "Team Boundless, please report to the hadron collider immediately for teleportation."

Alex took a deep breath as she tried to smile at the rest of the team. This was it; they were heading back to Earth. This wasn't how she was expecting her return to Earth to be, but she was with Boundless. It couldn't possibly be too bad.

The secret weapon capable of destroying the Dark One is buried on the moon. But dragons aren't meant to go to space ...Join the Alex and the Boundless in *To The Moon and Back*!

AUTHOR NOTES RAMY VANCE

APRIL 17, 2020

I couldn't make this up. I wish I could. I'd be a million, billion, trillionaire if could, but my mind simply couldn't conceive of such scenarios. And as such, I have been outdone by the greatest storyteller of all: Life.

At the peak of the Coronavirus crisis, my family got … lice.

"How?" you might ask. "Weren't you self-isolating?" you might ask. "Was someone cheating?" you might ask. Well, I can assure you that no one in the Vance household was sneaking away to have nefarious playdates, revelry and/or non-social distancing activities. We were diligent in our efforts to 'not see anyone.'

"But how did you get lice?"

The answer, I'm sad to say to say, was that my son must have picked it up on one of his last days of nursery – two weeks ago before we discovered it!

But we didn't detect it due to a hodgepodge of circumstances that were so coincidental I sometimes feel like a bit player in some farcical production.

Grandpa didn't get it. His lack of hair made his scalp a veritable nuclear wasteland for our dear lice friends.

I didn't get it. It seems that my hair is so thick that lice find my scalp the equivalent of a dense, deadly jungle ala 'Heart of Darkness' style.

As for the other three – they all got it. But my son seems impervious to discomfort. I once caught him running into a wall over and over again because – and I quote – "I see funny little lights when I hit my head hard enough."

As for grandma … her excuse was that her scalp always itched. "I'm old. Things are constantly breaking down, aching, itching, creaking. If I complained about it all, I'd never do anything else."

And as for my wife … she just had surgery and was put on blood pressure medication that has numerous side effect. Number 2 most common side effect: An itchy scalp (I'm not kidding).

Ultimately it was CoVid-19 that was the reason it took us 2 weeks to detect it. Four adults and two kids cooped up in a single household was a pressure cooker of discontent even when we can go outside at will. But with the quarantine in effect, you can imagine we all wanted to be on our best behaviour.

No one complained … much. We knew these were extreme circumstances and we tended to keep our bitching to things we could change. As a result … the three infected just kept it to themselves until one day the itching grew to an unbearable frenzy.

Shaving our heads was a blast. It's been awhile since I laughed so hard … and as memorable as I'm sure CoVid-19 will be, it will forever be overshadowed by the time we got lice and, as a family, shaved our heads.

Peace fellow humans. No doubt this situation is terrible. But just because it's terrible, doesn't mean it has to suck.

(And if you're reading this when Coronavirus is a distant memory … well, I hope my plight of lice put a smile on your face!)

Before

After

AUTHOR NOTES MICHAEL ANDERLE

APRIL 17, 2020

THANK YOU for reading our story!

We have a few of these planned, but we don't know if we should continue writing and publishing without your input.

Options include leaving a review, reaching out on Facebook to let us know and smoke signals.

Frankly, smoke signals might get misconstrued as low hanging clouds so you might want to nix that idea...

I don't cut hair... (And I've never had lice, so don't know anything about that.)

I used to have long hair when I was in college. It was that 'you aren't in your parents' home, I can have long hair and an earring' time during the 1980's. I shared this rejection of authority by growing my hair long, using hair bands while riding motorcycles.

Yes, I listened to heavy metal and had a Kawasaki EX500... They called it a sport-tourer, I called it fun and thankfully not the death of me.

It was the closest thing to sexy I *ever* had in my notoriously geek life. Except for something recently in the last five years, but that doesn't count.

I'm married. Owning sexy stuff while married takes the sexy out of it. I've lived through the young-family-has-a-van-to-drive days and now I'm in the older-life-kids-out-of-the-house-can-afford-more-expensive-toys days.

Back in the 80's, my hair got long enough that when I rode, I had to use a hair band or rubber band (which HURTS like an SOB trying to get it out of the hair) or spend twenty minutes cussing as I tried to pull a hairbrush through the tangles if I forgot.

I still flinch to this day thinking about pulling the hairbrush through my hair. I am empathetic to any dogs when you have to comb them and they have tangles. I try my best to keep away any pain.

Today I like to wear my hair much shorter because it takes less time to dry.

With the Pandemic, and not haircutting barbershops or anything available, I am trying new ways to style it.

Not very successfully mind you. I'm married, I only have one person to impress and she is usually looking at me strange. This would be a typical discussion.

Wife: "What is that hairstyle called?"

Me: "Keep it the @#%@# out of my face."

Wife: "… looks nice."

Well, she *SAID* looks nice. Her rolling eyes proclaimed she meant something else.

Ad Aeternitatem,

Michael Anderle

OTHER BOOKS BY THE AUTHORS

Other Middang3ard Books

Never Split The Party (01)
Late To the Party (02)
It's My Party (03)
Blue Hell And Alien Fire (04)

Death Of An Author: A Middang3ard Novella

Other Books by Ramy Vance

Mortality Bites Series
Keep Evolving Series
Fatebound Series
Welcome to the Dragon Show Series

Other Books by Michael Anderle

For a complete list of books by Michael Anderle, please visit:

www.lmbpn.com/ma-books/

All LMBPN Audiobooks are Available at Audible.com and iTunes. To see all LMBPN audiobooks, including those written by Michael Anderle please visit:

www.lmbpn.com/audible

CONNECT WITH THE AUTHORS

Connect with Ramy

Join Ramy's Newsletter to get a **FREE AUDIOBOOK!**
Join Ramy's FB Group: House of the GoneGod Damned!

Connect with Michael Anderle and sign up for his email list here:

Website: http://lmbpn.com

Email List: http://lmbpn.com/email/

Facebook:
www.facebook.com/TheKurtherianGambitBooks

www.ingramcontent.com/pod-product-compliance
Lightning Source LLC
Chambersburg PA
CBHW050157110726
47898CB00008B/2844